The Happiest Lion Cub This edition published in 2022 by Red Comet Press LLC, Brooklyn, NY

First published in 2021 under the title **Найщасливіше левеня** (Happiest Lion Cub) by Vydavnytstvo Staroho Leva (The Old Lion Publishing House), Lviv, Ukraine

Text & illustrations copyright © 2021 Oleksandr Shatokhin English Translation © 2022 Red Comet Press LLC

Translated by Zenia Tompkins

Library of Congress Control Number: 2022930014 ISBN (HB): 978-1-63655-038-1 ISBN (EBOOK): 978-1-63655-039-8

22 23 24 25 TLF 10 9 8 7 6 5 4 3 2 1

First Edition • Manufactured in China • RedCometPress.com

The Happiest Lion Cub

OLEKSANDR SHATOKHIN

Translated By
ZENIA TOMPKINS

Red Comet Press • Brooklyn

In the faraway
African savanna,

there lived an **UNUSUAL**
little lion cub.

A lion cub who **DREAMED** of becoming a musician.

"The **FUTURE** king of the savanna a **MUSICIAN**?"

"That's **UNHEARD** of!" the animals of the savanna gasped in hushed whispers.

The cub's father was **VERY** displeased.
Because a lion cub

OUGHT TO

spend his time on **REAL** lion things,
not go around making music!

A **REAL** lion ought to hunt.

And also roar **LOUDLY** and **EXPRESSIVELY!**

His father even composed a special list
of **VIRTUES** for the future king of the savanna.

Virtues of a Real Lion, Future King of the Savanna!

A real Lion ought to know how to:

- roar loudly
- hunt
- sit as if frozen
- maintain a regal silence
- observe carefully
- not laugh when he has the giggles
- not show fear when he's scared

A real lion ought to be:

- honest
- brave
- serious
- just
- considerate
- persistant
- hardy

and other such things...

Approved by King Lion

But the lion cub didn't want to hunt.
He **DREAMED** of playing in an **ORCHESTRA!**

He didn't want to roar like other lions.
Instead, he **LOVED** to sing.

No—no, the lion cub didn't want to be king.
He dreamed of all of Africa drifting off
to sleep to the sound of his **TENDER**
and **ENCHANTING** music.

The lion cub tried convincing his father of this,
but his father was unwavering:
"You're a **LION!** Your calling is to be the
KING OF THE SAVANNA! PERIOD!"

Oh, how sad it is
when no one **UNDERSTANDS** you.

It even started raining.

But wait, what are these **STRANGE** sounds he hears through the rattling of the rain?

As if someone was **CRYING** in the spooky, prickly thicket.

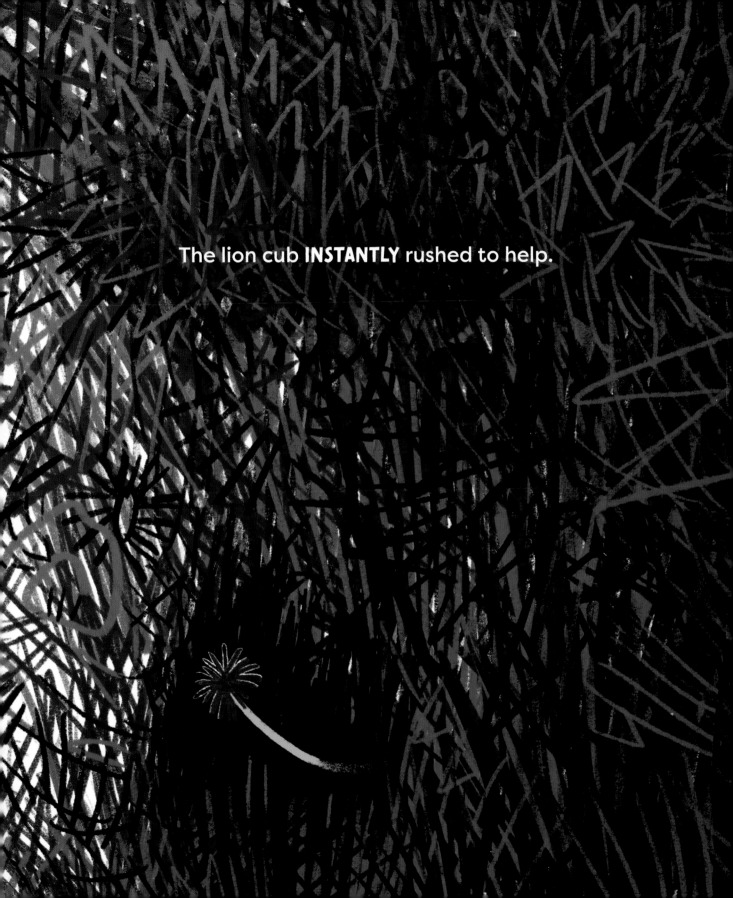

The lion cub **INSTANTLY** rushed to help.

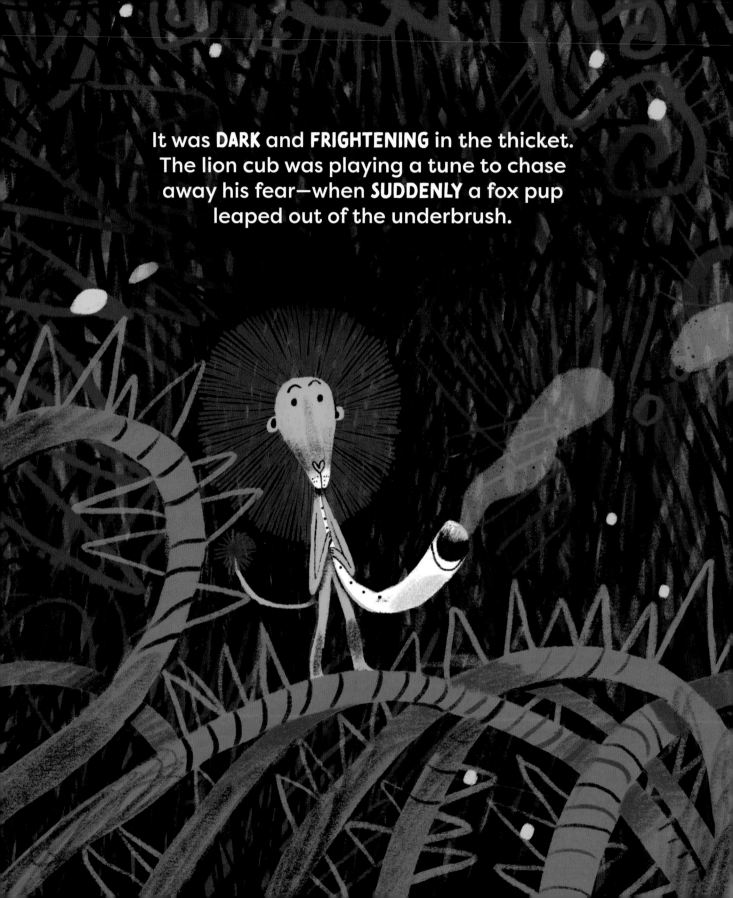

It was **DARK** and **FRIGHTENING** in the thicket. The lion cub was playing a tune to chase away his fear—when **SUDDENLY** a fox pup leaped out of the underbrush.

"How did you end up here?" asked the lion cub.
"I was hiding from the rain and got lost,"
replied the fox pup. "I **GOT SO SCARED!** When I heard
your song, I walked toward the sound.
Thank you for rescuing me, **BRAVE** lion!"

"IT WAS THE MUSIC! But now we need to find our way out of here," said the lion cub.

When the cub and pup
crawled out of the thicket,
they saw their parents.

The sounds of the music
had led them to this spot too.

King Lion finally understood
that his son had a **BIG** heart.
And that he was **BRAVE**, like a **REAL** lion.
And also an **INCREDIBLE MUSICIAN!**
And among lions, that's a rare thing.

Years passed. The lion cub grew up and became the **FIRST** musician king in Africa.

And he was the **HAPPIEST** king
because he could spend his life doing
what he had dreamed of most.